This one is for Mommy
Bernette Ford

For Trevor 'Rabbit' and Martin 'Mouse'
love from Sam Williams 'Dolit'

First American edition published in 2007
by Boxer Books Limited.

Distributed in the United States and Canada by
Sterling Publishing Co., Inc.
387 Park Avenue South, New York, NY 10016-8810

First published in Great Britain in 2007
by Boxer Books Limited.
www.boxerbooks.com

Text copyright © 2007 Bernette Ford
Illustrations copyright © 2007 Sam Williams

ISBN-13: 978-1-905417-34-6
ISBN-10: 1-905417-34-9

1 3 5 7 9 10 8 6 4 2

Printed in China

No More Bottles for Bunny!

Bernette Ford and Sam Williams

Boxer Books

Bunny has a bottle at mealtime.

Bunny has a bottle at nap time.

Bunny even has a bottle

when he goes out to play.

Ducky is having a tea party.

She has cookies on little plates.

She has make-believe tea

in a lovely teapot.

Piggy comes to the tea party.

Bunny wants to play, too.

He wants cookies and make-believe tea.

But Bunny is sucking on his bottle.

"I'm the mama," says Ducky.

She pours some tea into Piggy's mug.

She takes a bite of cookie.

Bunny sucks on his bottle.

Ducky takes a tiny sip of tea

from her shiny yellow ducky mug.

"Yummy!" says Ducky.

Bunny sucks on his bottle.

"I'm the daddy," says Piggy.

He takes a bite of cookie.

Bunny sucks on his bottle.

Piggy takes a long drink of tea

from his pink piggy mug.

"Mmm-m-m-m!" says Piggy.

Bunny stops sucking on his bottle.

Bunny holds out his bottle.

"Me, too," says Bunny.

"You can't have tea in a bottle!"

says Ducky.

"Bottles are for babies."

"I have an idea," says Piggy.

"You can be the baby."

Bunny shakes his head —

NO, NO, NO!

Bunny runs to the kitchen.

He tosses his bottle into the trash.

He waves.

"Bye-bye, bottle!" says Bunny.

"Where is your bottle, Bunny?"

asks Ducky.

"I'm not a baby anymore,"

says Bunny.

"I'm a big boy now!"

Bunny takes a bite of cookie.

He takes a long drink of tea

from his bright red bunny mug.

"Mmm-m-m-m!" he says.

"No more bottles for Bunny!"